The Hunt for
Anakin Skywalker
NOVEL

STAR WARS ADVENTURES

The Hunt for
Anakin Skywalker

Dave Wolverton

LUCAS BOOKS

SCHOLASTIC INC.

New York • Toronto • London • Auckland • Sydney
Mexico City • New Delhi • Hong Kong • Buenos Aires

ISBN 0-439-45887-0

12 11 10 9 8 7 6 5 4 3 2   3 4 5 6 7 8/0

Printed in the U.S.A.
First Scholastic printing, February 2000

The Hunt for
Anakin Skywalker

CHAPTER ONE

Sebulba was furious as he and his men searched the fortress of Gardulla the Hutt. He cursed Gardulla under his breath as he walked down the hallways.

The Ghostling children—slaves he'd worked hard to catch—had escaped from right under Gardulla's nose. Now, she was going to make Sebulba find them for her.

It was unfair. If they'd been on a world that was part of the Republic, Sebulba would have taken Gardulla to court. But there were no courts on Tatooine. Just Hutts with a lot more power than Sebulba. He would have to find the slaves and that meant work. If there was one thing Sebulba hated, it was work.

Sebulba's tracker, Djas Puhr, was walking behind him, along with the Dug, Khiss. Gondry, a greenish-tan Abyssin giant, lumbered down the hall toward Sebulba, head hanging. His moustache was long and gnarled. He acted like an overgrown kid as he punched the DOWN button on the turbolift.

Sebulba drew his heavy blaster and smiled wickedly. "Step away from the door," he said. Gondry looked at him, mouth wide in panic. "You'll never let another slave escape," Sebulba growled in Huttese.

"Hwaree!" Gondry said. He really did feel sorry. It was all his fault that the children escaped. He was supposed to be guarding them. But he'd left the room because some Jawas had told him to!

Sebulba fired, and a reddish bolt slammed into Gondry's stomach.

The giant's single yellow eye opened wide in pain. He blinked back a tear. "I hwaree," Gondry said in his thick accent as he slumped to the floor.

"Not as sorry as you're going to be!" Sebulba shouted. Sebulba's heart was pounding hard. He wanted to rip the giant to shreds, but Gondry's people were notoriously hard to hurt. They could regenerate limbs and heal their wounds in minutes.

Sebulba leaped upon the giant's chest and ripped out a handful of moustache hair. Gondry winced in pain.

Sebulba jabbed Gondry in the eye with his blaster and screamed, "I'm going to shoot you every day for a week until you find those children!"

Gondry threw a hand in front of his face to protect himself. Sebulba bit his wrist and, for a moment, they wrestled—Sebulba flailing and biting, Gondry trying to ward off the blows.

"Forgive me, boss, if I say this," Djas Puhr ventured, "but the more time you waste punishing Gondry, the harder it becomes to trail the Jawas who stole our slaves." The tall Sakiyan spoke gently, reasonably.

Sebulba scowled and got off Gondry. He felt worn-out, even after a little bit of a scuffle. It was too much like work.

"All right," Sebulba said. He stalked into the turbolift. Djas Puhr followed, along with Khiss, the hulking Dug. Gondry crawled in last.

Punishing the giant hadn't done any good. Sebulba had started out being mad. Now he was mad *and* tired. The elevator opened on the seventh level, the slave quarters. The lights were out in the deep shafts. Sebulba and his henchmen stepped into the hall. The hallway was carved of sandstone. Pipes overhead carried electric cables and cool air to the far reaches of the fortress.

A giant mora beetle sounded off its horn to their left. Sebulba got out of the elevator just as it turned and charged.

The enormous beetle thundered through the corridor on its ten legs. Sebulba couldn't see it.

Khiss brought up his blaster rifle and shot. Blaster fire illuminated the air. Khiss saw the huge black creature with green eyes rushing toward him. The blaster blew away chunks of chitin, and the dead beetle skidded to a halt just centimeters from Sebulba's foot.

Khiss took a small but powerful light from his belt and shined it to his right. Dead bugs littered the hall, and the smell of transmitter fire filled the air. A giant ghost spydr had spun a web at the end of the hall. It had already caught a two-headed effrikim worm, and was wrapping the poor worm in cords that were stronger than steel.

The Jawas who'd let the bugs out of their pens and freed the slaves had made a mess of Gardulla's fortress. Smoke was still rising in places.

They'd done a fine job.

Sebulba suddenly realized that he wasn't mad at Gondry anymore. He wasn't even angry at Gardulla.

It was the Jawas who had caused the problem —dirty, stinking, evil little Jawas with their bright glowing eyes! He hated them.

I know what I'll do, Sebulba thought. *I'll catch those Jawas and leave them out in a Sarlaac pit.*

He was imagining how much fun it would be when he reached the scene of the crime. The door was blown off the infirmary. Khiss shone his light into the room. It reflected off medical equipment and beds. Fortunately, there were no giant ghost spydrs running amok.

Djas Puhr entered first and sniffed the air. "The trail is growing cold," he said. "Gardulla's henchmen have been in here. The Gamorreans stunk up the room pretty bad."

"Can you smell the Jawas?" Sebulba asked. "I want the Jawas who did this."

The huge Sakiyan crept around the room, sniffing at the doorjamb, smelling the counters, hovering near the lock of the energy cage that had held the Ghostling children.

After several long minutes, he said, "Gondry, describe these Jawas for me."

Gondry was standing now, though he still looked shaken. The blast wound to his belly was healing.

"Uh, shwort," he said. "Hwave eyes thwat glow. Hwear robes."

"Are you sure they weren't humans?" Djas Puhr asked. "I smell two humans, a Twi'lek, and something else, some creature I'm not sure of."

"Too small to be hwumans," Gondry insisted.

"Children!" Khiss said. He began to growl deep in his throat. "Children!"

"What?" Sebulba asked.

"Yesterday I caught two slave children talking to the Ghostlings at the docking bay. I took some shots at them, but missed."

Sebulba gaped at his henchmen in surprise. Slave children had done this? *Slaves* had made a mess of Gardulla's fortress? How interesting. The Hutts offered rewards for anyone caught helping to free their slaves. The reward for these children might be enough to pay Sebulba for his trouble.

"If we catch them," Sebulba said, "we'll have to devise some special torture!"

"Not *if* we catch them," Djas Puhr said. "*When*." The Sakiyan tracker picked up something small from the floor and held it for the others to inspect. It was a flake of green skin from a Twi'lek.

"Run it through a scanner," Sebulba said. "When we get a match, this one will lead us to the others."

CHAPTER TWO

"Did you girls hear the news?" Madam Vansitt asked that morning at her Charm Academy. "Some children tried to free some slaves last night at Gardulla's palace. Many of the tunnels are in ruins."

"Who would do such a silly thing?" Ado Mura asked. She was a human girl with dark skin.

Pala glanced this way and that. All twelve of the girls in Pala's class looked at one another in total astonishment. She forced her head-tails to be still, so that she wouldn't betray her anxiety. She hoped that the others would imagine that they saw just as much astonishment in her golden eyes. As a student, she was being trained to be a spy. But she'd never felt as much apprehension as she did right now.

"I don't know," Madam Vansitt answered. "But they will not get away with it. They found a flake of skin at the scene. It was Twi'lek skin...."

Perhaps Madam Vansitt added that bit just as an item of curiosity. Four students in the room were Twi'lek. But few of Pala's people lived on Tatooine, and fewer still were children. In fact, in the city of Mos Espa, most of those children were sitting in this room.

She suspects one of us, Pala realized. Madam Vansitt glanced around, letting her eyes rest on each girl in turn.

They'd been learning various subtle means of sabotaging droids. Pala was sitting at a table with a droid's positronic sensor array in her hand. She set the array down carefully, along with a spanner.

Pala had spent the whole morning filled with anxiety. She'd been sold to Lord Tantos, one of the vilest pirates in the galaxy. That was enough to terrify her. But after her little escapade last night...

Madam Vansitt glanced at Pala. She was a large woman who wore her lipstick just so. Her teeth were filed to sharp points, and when she smiled they showed like pearly daggers in her mouth. Now there was a hint of a smile in her eyes, but none showed on her bloodred lips.

Pala was very careful not to reveal the turmoil building inside her.

"You all know the punishment for such a crime," Madam Vansitt said. "Death."

She said it as she let her glance rest on Pala.

"It is a just punishment," Madam Vansitt continued in her normal lecture tone. "As I've told you a thousand times, *Punishment for a crime is a price that only the stupid are forced to pay*. If smart girls—my girls—commit a crime, they should never get caught!"

The girls all began chattering innocently. Crimes were committed on Tatooine every day, and Madam Vansitt almost always took time to discuss them in her classes. If the crime went well, she would talk about why the plot had succeeded. If the crime went wrong, she'd criticize the performance and analyze why it had failed.

"Girls," Madam Vansitt suddenly said in a casual tone, "what was the first mistake that these children made?"

Pala's friend Gola raised a hand. "Four of them went to do one person's job!"

"That's right," Madam Vansitt agreed. "Never tell anyone about a crime you intend to commit. An accomplice will always inform on you. There are machines that can extract information from even the most unwilling prisoner.

"In this case, one of the children left a flake of skin at the scene. The child may have brushed against a door, or torn it off in a scuffle. In any case, the damage is done. The scanner will identify the criminal by nightfall, and he or she will be in the hands of Gardulla. Once that happens, Gardulla will wring the truth from him or her, and everyone that was involved will pay the ultimate price."

Gola asked, "What do you think Gardulla will do?"

Madam Vansitt frowned. "Ah, that's so horrible, I dare not say...."

"Oh, come on," the children all begged. "Please?"

"Well," Madam Vansitt said, "the last time a thief tried to steal one of her slaves, Gardulla made a throw rug from his skin. She'll want to outdo herself this time, though."

"Ew!" the girls all called out, making disgusted faces.

Pala couldn't help it. A shiver of terror swept through her, and her head-tails began to lash.

Madam Vansitt's eyes flicked toward her.

She knows, Pala thought. *She knows, and she's not going to say anything.*

Madam Vansitt suddenly smiled broadly, and her sharp teeth looked as if they would cut through her lips.

"So," she said, "let's imagine for a moment that one of you had committed the crime and knew that you had only hours left to live. What would you do?"

The girls all looked at one another. There was only one possible answer: Escape! But slaves never talked about that in front of their owners.

"I'd try to escape," Pala said boldly.

"Hmmm…" Madam Vansitt shook her head. "That's not very practical when you have a transmitter hidden in you. All your owner has to do is push a button, and…"

But in this case, Pala thought, *my owner can't push that button. By doing it, she'd blow my brains out—and that means that the other slaves who helped commit the crime might never be caught. No, she needs me alive.*

"Maybe you could hope to get sold to someone off-planet," Pala suggested.

She was thinking furiously. There would surely be a reward for her capture. But how much was Pala worth as a slave? Was it possible that Pala was worth more to Madam Vansitt alive than dead? Would Madam Vansitt go so far as to help Pala escape?

Pala didn't believe that.

"Ah, that would be a nice fantasy," Madam Vansitt said. "And in your case, it's almost true. You're to be sold tomorrow, and if Lord Tantos decided to pick you up a day early, then your life might be spared. But I doubt it. He has to do business with the Hutts, after all. And he wouldn't want a slave that he couldn't trust. No, he'd wring the information from you himself, and then turn you over to Gardulla, so that she might have her fun...."

Pala kept thinking. *She knows what I did, but she's not doing anything about it. She could tell Gardulla herself, get in her good graces....*

"I'm afraid," Madam Vansitt said, "that the slave who did this is as good as dead. It would be a shame if it were one of you. After all, here at Madam Vansitt's Charm Academy, we have a high reputation to uphold. We have a tradition to maintain."

Reputation. That's it! Pala realized. Madam Vansitt knew what she'd done, and as soon as the rest of the galaxy found out, it would tarnish her reputation.

One of her girls, one of the slaves she was training as a spy, was stupid enough to get caught.

That would hurt the academy. It would cost Madam Vansitt sales, hurt the school's reputation for decades to come. It might even ruin her financially.

But if that same slave managed to escape…the school's reputation would be salvaged. Pala could almost imagine the things that would be said. "Did you hear about that slave girl Madam Vansitt was training? She broke into Gardulla's fortress and stole some slaves right under her nose, then just disappeared. Madam Vansitt sure knows how to train them!"

Madam Vansitt would lose a fortune if Pala died. She'd make a fortune if she escaped.

But even if Madam Vansitt wanted to help Pala escape, she couldn't. She'd get in too much trouble if anyone found out.

So Pala had to do it on her own. She had to figure out how to get off Tatooine. And once she was off, she could never let herself be caught again.

She pretended to work on the positronic sensor array, and thought frantically.

She grew restless throughout the day, and hoped that Madam Vansitt would let her out of class. It wasn't until midafternoon that her slave-master touched her on the shoulder and said, "Pala, are you all packed for tomorrow?"

"Not all the way," Pala lied.

"Go make sure that you've packed up everything. Then say good-bye to your friends."

Pala bolted for her room, and grabbed her bags. Madam Vansitt's last words kept echoing in her mind. "Say good-bye to your friends. *Say good-bye.*"

CHAPTER THREE

Djas Puhr wasn't content to wait for the results of the sequencer scan.

Sakiyans are born to hunt. His eyes let him see his prey in total darkness. His keen ears let him hear the little gravel-maggots crawling under the hot stones of Tatooine. His sense of smell was so strong that few slaves ever eluded him for long.

He was one of the best trackers in the galaxy.

Djas Puhr had caught the scent of two human children in the infirmary. If he ever smelled one of them again, he'd recognize the scent. The thrill of the hunt was upon him.

He took along a seeker, a droid that could detect smells even better than he could. The black droid, which hovered on little repulsor-lift engines, moved easily through tight spots. With its powerful thrusters and little stabilizer fins, it could travel much faster than a man could run. It would be tireless in its hunt.

In the depths of Gardulla's palace, there was a counter where one of the children had picked up some transmitters—transmitters that had later been used to destroy dozens of tunnels and battle droids. Gardulla would be glad to learn who had done that.

"Droid, can you smell the human who last touched this counter?" Djas Puhr asked.

"Yes," the droid answered. "I recognize a scent: male, human, child."

"Precisely," Djas Puhr said. "Let's find him."

With that, the droid's repulsor-lift engines began to whir, and it carefully spun, seeking its prey.

* * *

"Bah," Watto cursed at Anakin. "You're no good to me this way! What's wrong? Are you sick?"

The Toydarian softly flapped around Anakin in the junkyard behind his shop, looking at the boy from all angles. Anakin was one of Watto's most valuable slaves. He didn't want Anakin to be sick.

"Maybe," Anakin said. He was worried and exhausted. He'd worked all day yesterday, and then he'd helped to rescue the Ghostling children on top of that. He hadn't slept all night.

Now he couldn't concentrate on work. All morning he'd been looking through piles of junk for a new control cable shock absorber for Watto's Podracer.

"Don't get sick on me," Watto warned him. "Your work will just pile up."

"I—I couldn't sleep last night," Anakin confessed. "I found something at the Jawas' market yesterday. I think it's a box of some kind. I couldn't get it open."

"Let me see, eh?" Watto demanded.

Anakin hadn't meant to show it to him. He was afraid that it might be valuable, and Watto would take it away. But he needed some excuse for being tired, and he really didn't know how to open the box.

He reached into the pocket of his robe, fished out the cube, and held it up for Watto's inspection.

The Toydarian landed and stood scrutinizing the cube for a moment. He studied the words written on each side of the cube. They were written in some language that Anakin had never seen. He looked at the images.

"Hmmm..." Watto said, puzzled. "Old. Very old, I think. One, two thousand years."

He squinted at the thing from all angles. "Looks solid. What makes you think it's a box, eh?"

"The weight," Anakin said. "It's hollow. I'm sure there's something inside."

"Eh, I don't see any seams! It's no box." Watto picked up a powerful magnifying glass that he often used to inspect datachips. "Hmmm...maybe."

Anakin hadn't been able to spot any seams, either. Still, he felt sure that it was a box.

"Nah," Watto said, tossing the cube back to Anakin. "It's a die, I think—probably for some old game of chance. Worthless junk, eh?"

Anakin was glad that Watto thought it was worthless. That way, he wouldn't take it.

"Go, now," Watto continued. "Get some sleep for a few hours. But I expect you to work all the harder when you wake up!"

"All right!" Anakin exclaimed. "Thank you!"

Watto waved him away, and Anakin ran out of the junk shop and into the blinding sunlight. He raced around a ronto that was coming to the door—ridden by one of the Weequays who wanted to sell Watto some junk. Then he dodged up the streets through an obstacle course of eopies, droids, beings, and vehicles.

Mos Espa was a crowded city of buildings the color of sand. Most of the buildings were shaped like domes, to withstand the sometimes deadly desert winds.

He hadn't gone far when he saw Kitster, Pala, and Dorn, all sitting near Jira's stand.

Immediately, Anakin knew that something was wrong. He could see fear in his friends' faces.

He didn't even bother to buy a drink from Jira. He sat down and asked, "What happened?"

Dorn, a Bothan who Jabba was training as a spy, forced his long eyebrows to lay back flat against his temples, as if he weren't nervous at all. He whispered, "They're onto us. Gardulla found out that four kids broke into her fortress, and the Hutts are offering a reward. They've got a sample of Pala's skin, and they should have her identified by tonight."

In his most terrible nightmares, Anakin couldn't have imagined any news as bad. He looked into the faces of his friends, and didn't know what to say.

They were all going to be caught...and punished. It wasn't fair.

He hadn't done anything wrong—none of them had done anything wrong. They'd only been trying to help rescue the Ghostling children, young kids who had been kidnapped from their homes. If anyone should have been punished, it was Gardulla and Sebulba.

"What are we going to do?" Anakin asked. His throat was tight.

Suddenly Jira appeared at his back, throwing a cool shadow over the table. She put a green-colored fruit drink down on the table in front of him. "Why don't you children come out of the sun? It's much cooler in my apartment."

"Uh, no," Anakin said. He didn't want Jira to hear what they were talking about.

She leaned close, and her gray hair, coiled together like rags, brushed his neck. "I think you should. Gardulla has a bounty on four children who tried to free her slaves last night. Someone might look at you four and get the wrong idea."

Anakin looked up into Jira's dark face. She was a kind woman, as poor as the poor can get. She wore the same clothes every day, and she didn't charge much more for her drinks than what they cost to make. But she'd read his face well enough. He glanced over at her little cart and saw that she had already locked it up.

"Come on." She turned her broad back and walked toward her apartment. One by one the children followed.

She led them through a narrow alley where the blistering suns of Tatooine did not reach. Her apartment didn't have a lock. It didn't even have a moisture seal to keep the air humid inside. When she reached it, she shooed away a pair of Jawas who were peeking through the door.

When they got inside, Anakin saw why she didn't bother to have a lock. There was very little furniture—only a bed and a couple of shelves. The nooks built into the pour-stone walls didn't have any of the normal electronics in them.

Either she didn't feel that she had anything worth protecting, or thieves had stolen it all already. She didn't seem to care. Anakin thought of all the times that Jira had given him drinks for free, and he felt embarrassed.

"Come," she said, "have a seat." She motioned to the floor, and sat down cross-legged on a ragged pillow. The kids all sat down around her. Jira wasn't really a big woman. She was taller than the kids, large of bone. But in the bare room she had a commanding presence. Or maybe she dominated the room simply because she was older than all of the kids in it put together.

"Now, we talk," she said. "What were you thinking, trying to free those slaves?"

"They aren't slaves," Anakin protested. "They're kids, all younger than us—Ghostlings. Sebulba caught them on Datar, a Republic world. Gardulla wants to put them in her garden because they look pretty. But they'll just die there. We thought—we hoped we could save them."

"Hmmm," Jira said thoughtfully. "Ghostlings are very frail. It was kind of you to try to help. But now, how are you going to save yourselves?"

"I...," Pala started to say. But she didn't finish the sentence. She didn't have a plan.

"And what about the Ghostlings?" Jira asked. "Breaking them out of their cages isn't the same thing as setting them free. What if Gardulla sets off their transmitters?"

"She didn't have time to install them," Anakin said quickly. "That's why we had to break them out last night. We couldn't wait."

"I see," Jira said. "So how are you going to get them back to Datar?"

"I was up thinking about that all night," Kitster admitted, but he didn't have an answer.

"We might be able to stow them on a ship that is heading toward Datar." Dorn put in.

But Datar was a long way from Mos Espa. Anakin doubted that he'd ever find a ship that was going straight there.

"I see," Jira said. "So you broke them out of the fortress, hoping to send them home later."

She looked very worried and very thoughtful. Her brown eyes flicked around the room, resting on each of the children. "There are ways to get off-planet," she continued in a dangerous tone. "Sometimes, slaves disappear and are never found. It can be arranged, if you know the right people."

"Do you know someone who can help?" Anakin asked. Instantly he realized that he shouldn't have. That wasn't the kind of question that a smart person would answer.

She shook her head. "I know someone who knows someone. He can get children off of Tatooine. But it costs a lot of money—money for transport, and money for bribes."

"The children's parents will pay, I'll bet," Dorn said quickly. "Princess Arawynne's parents will pay."

"Hah!" Jira barked in laughter. "Maybe they would at that. But it would take weeks to contact them, if we go through normal channels. We don't have weeks. Pala needs to go *now*! So, it will take money. Lots of money. And as you can see, I don't have any." She gestured expansively to her nearly empty apartment, and Anakin suddenly wondered: Was she so poor because she'd given everything she had to good causes?

"I've got a little money," Pala offered.

"I'm sure you do," Jira replied. "But it takes *a lot*. It takes money to pay for fuel for a ship, and for weapons. And we must pay extra, to make it worthwhile to those who might help us. This is not something that can be arranged by sundown. Gardulla will be coming for you before then."

"I can try hiding," Pala said.

"With that transmitter in you," Jira cautioned, "you'll need to hide very well. Otherwise, the masters will find you fast."

"If she hides underground," Kitster said, "the transmitter signal might not get through."

Jira shook her head. "The masters will think of that. They'll check the sewers and underground tunnels right off."

"I know," Anakin said. "I can make a signal jammer, to help keep them from finding her."

"Can you do that?" Pala asked, obviously worried.

"Sure I can. I can make one so good that you won't even be able to find yourself!" Anakin was already planning it. All he needed was a transmitter and a computer to randomly send out signals at high power, effectively masking any signals that Pala's transmitter sent.

"What if the masters just blow her up?" Kitster asked.

"They won't," Pala said. "They want me alive, so that they can force me to tell them who was with me when the Ghostling Children were freed." Pala looked at each of her friends. "But I promise, no matter what happens, I'll never tell."

Dorn threw both of his pointed ears back and arched his brows so that the long hairs rose up questioningly. "Jira, I've heard how much it costs to smuggle a slave off of this planet. You're talking ten thousand wupiupi per person. We'll never get that kind of money!"

"There is always hope," Jira said. "Most slaves have a *little* money. All together, maybe it will be enough."

Anakin studied Jira's weathered face to see if she believed it. Collecting so much money would be almost impossible. He couldn't imagine that Jira could do it without getting caught.

"Now, I must get to work," Jira said, wringing her gnarled hands. "Pala, you'll have to hide. But the rest of you must go home and act normal. Don't walk in a group. Go out one by one. Come back after dark, and I will tell you whether the news is good or bad."

I've got to get to work, too, Anakin realized. *If I don't get that signal jammer to Pala fast, we could all end up dead.*

CHAPTER FOUR

For most of the day, the seeker droid whisked through Gardulla's fortress with Djas Puhr following. The scent of the boy was everywhere. He'd climbed through air vents, used long-neglected tunnels, and hidden in dark corners.

But finally his trail led through a vent in Gardulla's pool room out to the desert. The afternoon suns were blistering hot, and the light reflected off the white sands. Djas Puhr saw best at night. He had to put on a dark visor to see anything at all in daylight.

From markings in the sand, Djas Puhr decided that the children had ridden into the desert on some sort of vehicles, probably crude sand skimmers.

The skimmers left no scent at all. His seeker lost the trail a dozen times.

But the children had taken a direct path toward Mos Espa. They'd traveled through a narrow canyon where razor moss clung to the rocks and white funnel flowers hid in the shadows.

Once Djas Puhr reached Mos Espa, the scent of the boy would be easy to locate. The seeker would lead Djas Puhr to his home.

Eagerly, the tracker followed the droid. He warned it not to get ahead. He wanted to be there when the seeker found its quarry.

The seeker led him to the market, where dead animals hung in tempting displays and restaurant patrons sat beneath awnings to eat. People from a hundred worlds crowded the streets outside the spaceport.

Suddenly the seeker flashed a red warning light. "Target acquired, one hundred meters ahead— human boy, walking away from us."

Djas Puhr peered through the crowd of people, droids, and animals. The blinding suns of Tatooine baffled his vision even with a visor on.

A hundred meters ahead, he saw a blond-haired boy ambling away, head down in thought, and he was totally unaware of the danger.

Djas Puhr whispered into his handheld communicator. "Sebulba, target acquired. Repeat, target acquired. In the market."

The answer came back over the communicator. "We'll be right there."

At this point, you must decide whether to continue reading this adventure, or to play your own adventure in the Star Wars Adventures *The Hunt for Anakin Skywalker* Game Book.

To play your own adventure, turn to the first page of the Game Book and follow the directions you find there.

To continue reading this adventure, turn the page!

CHAPTER FIVE

Anakin split up from his friends before leaving Jira's. It was too dangerous for them to walk together.

He went back to Watto's and quickly made the signal jammer for Pala. It wasn't hard. Watto sold signal jammers all the time. Mostly pirates used them to jam communications when they attacked their victims. Those kinds of jammers were huge.

But Pala needed something small, something she could wear around her neck. So Anakin made a little signal jammer and put it on a thin cord. A piece of carved jinapoor over the top made it look like a slave's necklace.

He hoped it would work. It *had* to work!

And he had to get it to Pala soon. Gardulla might be able to identify her any minute.

Anakin felt desolate. Pala had been one of his best friends for as long as he could recall. He and Kitster and Pala had all been kept in Gardulla's fortress as children. He couldn't imagine life without her.

Things looked bleak.

Anakin had a strange sense that he was being followed. He turned and glanced down the path behind him. The road was full of people, droids, and animals. He didn't see any sign of danger.

Still, he couldn't be too safe. He turned off the road and went through a cantina that Sebulba *never* went to. Lots of his enemies hung out there—other racers that Sebulba had tried to cheat or kill. Anakin saw Mars Guo and Teemto Pagalies. The aliens paid no attention as Anakin skipped to the back door.

When he got out into the suns, he went a couple of blocks, ducked into a drainage pipe, and crawled through a narrow grate a block away.

That ought to throw off anyone who tries to follow me, Anakin thought. Then his mind returned to Pala.

It was up to Anakin to save her. But even if she lived, he'd never see her again. He'd stay a slave on Tatooine. She'd have to hide out among the stars.

He needed money to get her free.

He had a little money. Every slave got paid something—at least enough to purchase food. Sometimes Anakin would find a coin or a credit chip. Sometimes he traded little things he found to the Jawas and made more money.

If Watto ever discovered how much he had, Anakin figured that the Toydarian would stop giving him any at all. Masters tried to keep slaves poor.

Anakin had been saving it for something special. For as long as he could remember, Anakin had dreamed that someday he'd save enough to buy his mother's freedom. Yet even with all his saving, Anakin didn't think he'd have enough money for many years to come.

Now he'd have to give it all to Jira, to help Pala and the Ghostling children.

His mother would go on waiting for her freedom.

She's good at that, Anakin thought. *After all, she's had lots of practice. She's been waiting her whole life.*

These thoughts were circling in his head as he ambled toward Jira's apartment, through the afternoon crowd, wishing for sleep.

Suddenly a Jawa bumped into him. The Jawa pushed a robe into his hands and said in a familiar voice, "Don't get caught looking behind you!"

"Dorn?" Anakin asked in surprise. He couldn't see his friend's face beneath the deep robe.

"Follow me!" Dorn said.

"Where?"

But Dorn didn't answer. He just shoved his way through the crowd in his Jawa disguise.

Anakin's senses became alert. *Don't get caught looking behind you,* Dorn had said. Someone was after him! Fear made the hairs on the back of his neck prickle. Here in the market there were a hundred places to hide.

Dorn ducked around a corner, behind a stall where a vendor sold power generators for vaporators and pulled Anakin behind him.

Anakin glanced back. Striding purposefully through the crowd behind him was a tall man with a large skull and green-black skin—a Sakiyan tracker. Just in front of the Sakiyan floated a seeker droid.

The Sakiyan was stalking toward his hiding place.

"Get dressed and follow me!" Dorn said and ran up the street.

Anakin threw on the cloak, a simple brown Jawa robe, hoping that the disguise might protect him for a moment. He scrambled along in Dorn's tracks, but his friend had gotten ahead of him.

He ran to the outskirts of town, to the scrap market, where hundreds of Jawas were milling in the streets. There were droids and people all around, and huge displays of junk thrown out on tarps on the ground.

But in that sea of Jawas, where had Dorn gone?

* * *

Sebulba piloted a landspeeder through the crowded streets of Mos Espa. He was riding into town from the south, at the edge of a scrap market where Jawas had set up little displays and were selling junk they'd collected in the desert.

Eopies milled through the crowd, looking for things to eat. Battered droids ambled about, displaying themselves for any who bothered to look.

Normally, this street was pretty clear. But once each year the Jawas came in vast numbers.

A dewback ridden by Jawas crossed the path in front of him. Sebulba had to stop for the giant reptile. The Jawas were dragging a sled through town, loaded with an old rocket engine.

Sebulba shouted at them to hurry. He checked the setting on his blaster. He moved it to STUN. When he caught the boy he was looking for, he didn't want to kill him outright. Gardulla would want to spend a few days torturing him first. He laid the blaster in the seat beside him where he'd be able to grab it quickly.

The dewback stopped ahead of him. Four Weequays on rontos were coming from the opposite direction, and for a moment the intersection became blocked. The Weequays shouted at the Jawas to move their dewback. The Jawas shouted in return.

One of the Weequays raised an old blaster rifle and shook it over his head, threatening. The Jawas on the dewback drew their own blasters.

"Get out of my way!" Sebulba screamed at the whole lot of them.

Sebulba's comlink came on. "The boy is coming in your direction!"

Sebulba couldn't see down the street ahead. The rontos and dewback blocked the view.

Suddenly there was a movement to Sebulba's right. A Jawa rushed from the crowd beside him, reached into Sebulba's landspeeder, and grabbed his blaster.

"Hey, nice blaster! Can I borrow it?" The voice wasn't a Jawa's—it was human! The child grabbed the blaster and fired into a ronto.

"Hey, lucky shot!" the kid said. He tossed the blaster back to Sebulba, then rolled underneath the landspeeder.

The ronto wasn't wounded. The blaster was set on stun and didn't hurt the creature—it only made it furious. The ronto bellowed and swung its great head in rage. It knocked over a fruit stand. The Weequays on its back began to shout. They clung to the rampaging monster for dear life.

The street filled with screams of terror. The Jawas began firing their ion blasters into the air, trying to drive the ronto off.

"What?" Sebulba shouted. It had all happened so fast! He grabbed his blaster by the barrel. It was still hot. He flipped it in the air and caught it by the handle.

He tried to look under his landspeeder, to see where the pesky child was hiding.

A blaster bolt tore through the seat next to him. The Weequays were shooting at him! They thought that *he'd* shot their ronto.

Sebulba looked up and shouted in Huttese. The ronto swung its mighty head, slammed into the dewback, and turned its angry eyes on Sebulba's land-speeder. It charged.

Sebulba threw his landspeeder into reverse.

I'll kill that pesky child, Sebulba thought.

Another shot from the Weequays almost hit him. Sebulba snapped off a return shot. His landspeeder stirred up a cloud of sand as it whipped back through the narrow streets, faster than any ronto could run. Sebulba gripped his blaster and watched the street.

Had the kid run off through the crowd while Sebulba was distracted? He looked around wildly for a sign of the fleeing child, but didn't see him.

The ronto kept charging, but Sebulba had a racer's reflexes. He quickly outpaced the monster. The dewback roared in anger, dragging the huge engine off in a rush. The intersection was in chaos.

Sebulba backed around a corner and snickered in delight. He actually admired any kid who could cause so much trouble.

A call came in over his communicator. "Master," Djas Puhr said, "the boy is heading for the Podracer hangar. He'll be hiding in there."

Sebulba grinned wickedly. The hangar was a familiar place. No doubt, the silly child would try to hide in the cockpit of one of the Podracers. "Perfect! I'm almost there."

Dorn clung to the bottom of Sebulba's racer and grinned to himself. He'd left Anakin just a block up the street. Now Sebulba was going to give him a ride to the hangar!

Anakin stood at the edge of the scrap market for a moment, gazing at a thousand Jawas, wondering where Dorn might have gone.

A drink stand stood to the left above him. It was set on crates, and the Jawas had to climb up to get drinks.

At the top of the steps was a counter where three Jawas were dipping ewers into buckets of ganno juice, then selling cups of the syrupy black juice as fast as possible.

Humans hated ganno juice. It tasted bitter and made their sinuses swell.

As Anakin glanced around, he saw one Jawa up on the stand pull back its hood. Pala!

"Pala, I've got your *thing*!"

"Not now," she mouthed. She glanced to the south, toward the Podracer hangar, silently telling him to go that way. She mouthed one more word. "Hurry!"

He ran toward the hangar.

CHAPTER SIX

Djas Puhr was racing down the street through the Jawas' scrap market, trying to keep up with the seeker.

He'd had a hard time tracking the boy. Somehow, the child must have recognized that he was being followed. The little detour through the Racer's Edge Cantina had turned into an adventure.

He'd been detained for a moment by one of Sebulba's rivals. Djas Puhr shot the fellow quickly, then came searching for the blond-haired boy, but the child had disappeared. It took all of Djas Puhr's tracking skills to find him again.

Now he saw the boy ahead, running for his life, the only Jawa in the scrap market crowd in a hurry. He shouted over his comlink, "The boy is running for the Podracer hangar. He'll be hiding in there."

The seeker thrummed in the air above the narrow streets. It paused for a second, waiting for Djas Puhr to catch up.

Suddenly, from a high counter off to the right, a Jawa threw a bucket of dark fluid over its shoulder. The syrupy stuff hit the seeker droid full on and dripped all over it.

As the black juice oozed from his droid, Djas Puhr recognized the bitter scent of ganno. The stuff made his sinuses burn as if he were breathing acid.

The seeker buzzed to a halt.

Djas Puhr shouted to the droid, "Are you all right?"

"There's ganno juice on my olfactory sensors. I can't smell a thing!" the seeker said.

Djas Puhr rubbed at the juice, to keep it from seeping into the droid's electronics.

He heard a cry of outrage from the Jawas at the drink stand. For half a second, he had imagined that the Jawa had thrown the juice by accident, that it was simply tossing away some bad juice.

But now he realized that the Jawa had hurled a whole bucket on purpose. It wasn't an accident. It was an attack!

One of the children did this!

He drew his blaster, glanced up at the stand. But there had to be thirty Jawas and they all looked alike to him. Djas Puhr studied them feverishly.

"Who threw that?" he demanded, hoping that the Jawas would point out the culprit.

One of the Jawas spun around.

"Want seconds?" a girl asked. A second bucket of ganno juice hurtled through the air. It splashed over his visor. The smell was overwhelming.

Djas Puhr threw down his visor, trying to get the ganno juice as far away from himself as possible.

The blazing lights of Tatooine seemed to flare. He squinted painfully up at the drink stand, at the mass of Jawas shouting, outraged. His attacker jumped down behind the booth.

He squinted, trying to see well enough to shoot in the fierce sunlight. But without his dark visor, tears of pain blinded him.

The attacker was getting away!

CHAPTER SIX

CHAPTER SEVEN

Anakin raced into the Podracer hangar. The Pods and their engines were backed against the walls, stacked in storage.

The big Boonta Eve Race was still a week away, and only a couple of mechanic droids were working right now. Watto's old blue Podracer was there, but it wasn't in running shape. Anakin ran for it.

Down the line of racers, Kitster shouted, "Don't take that! If you fly it, everyone will know it's you. Try this one!" It was Sebulba's racer.

Anakin stopped at Watto's Podracer just long enough to grab his goggles.

He ran toward Kitster, worries nagging at him. Each Podracer in the hangar was built differently, customized for the driver. All of the racers but Watto's were built for aliens, some of whom had more limbs than Anakin, or were twice his size. He needed a racer built for someone short, with two arms and two legs.

Kitster was probably right. Sebulba's would be the best fit.

He ran to the orange racer. Kitster was sitting on the hood. He was already flipping buttons.

"Come on, Anakin. I've got the engines warm."

Anakin climbed into the cockpit and found Sebulba's goggles on the seat, along with some spanners. He threw them onto the floor. Kitster flipped on the controls. The telemetry and control console lit up. The Tradium power fluid levels were full; coolant levels looked to be within safety range. Stabilizers and altitude adjusters seemed functional.

Anakin flipped on the power to the repulsors. The repulsor-lift motors began to hum. The cockpit and engines all shuddered, then lifted into the air.

"Okay, get out of here," Anakin told Kitster. "I don't want you to get in trouble."

"No way," Kitster argued, squeezing in tightly beside him. "I'm coming with you! We're all in this together."

Anakin fished into his pocket for the signal jammer. "Give this to Pala."

"Not until we get rid of that seeker droid!" Kitster said.

Anakin flipped on the control power generator and the energy binders. A hot-pink flash, like lightning, erupted between the engines. The binders sent out powerful magnetic bursts that held the huge engines together.

"You've helped me enough," Anakin argued.

"Don't be stupid," Kitster said. "You're not out of this yet."

Anakin didn't have time to debate. He quickly studied Sebulba's control panel. It didn't make sense. There were too many buttons and switches.

He didn't know what all of them could do. He began playing with the air intake vents, making sure that they opened and closed properly on each engine. He wasn't used to the huge Collor Pondrat Plug-F Mammoth racing engines and their odd air intake system.

He wasn't done with his preflight check when the seeker droid appeared, whisking through the door.

The droid fired a stun dart that zipped over Anakin's head.

Anakin and Kitster ducked into the cockpit.

The droid skewed to the left and emitted a shower of sparks. Anakin saw now that the droid was damaged. A thin trail of blue-gray smoke issued from the diabolical machine. And black liquid was dripping from it. Some of the liquid must have dribbled into its housing, shorting its electric circuits.

Anakin grabbed the Podracer's controls. Sebulba had longer arms than Anakin. His throttle was up higher, and his racer had a much smaller duraplex windscreen on the front of it. Everything about the Podracer felt just a little wrong to Anakin.

Anakin twisted the throttle, and the engines roared to life. In the confines of the hangar, the noise was the sound of a thousand storms.

The wounded seeker rapidly shot toward him. Anakin knew he had to get rid of the droid. It had his scent!

Anakin fed the engines power, and they lurched forward from a dead stop to a hundred kilometers per hour. He aimed the Podracer at the droid.

Too late, the seeker recognized the danger. Its little repulsor-lift engines hummed to a stop, and for one second it hovered. Anakin's Podracer hurtled toward it.

Sparks erupted from the seeker's housing in a flurry. It tried to back up.

In less than a second, the huge Podracer engines straddled the droid, and Anakin rammed the droid with the energy binders.

For a human, touching the binder field left a limb paralyzed for a few hours. For the droid it was deadly. The powerful magnetic fields instantly fused its every component. Hot-pink threads of energy punched through the seeker, burning holes in its housing. The powerful magnetism scrambled the droid's positronic brains. Power cells inside the droid erupted in blue sparks, and the whole seeker burst into flames.

The Podracer itself slammed into the droid at 150 kilometers per hour. The droid shattered under the impact and sent flaming shards of metal in a thousand directions.

Podracers weren't made to negotiate hangars. One of the huge engines slammed into a repair droid that was working on Neva Kee's Podracer. The droid was hurled into a wall.

The Podracer swung like a pendulum from the jarring impact. It hit the left wall, then bounced right, scattering pit droids.

Now the Podracer was hurtling toward the hangar entrance at 230 kilometers per hour. The door wasn't open wide enough to get through, and Anakin didn't have time to stop.

Only the pod was small enough to make it through the door. Sebulba's oversized engines were going to crash into the wall!

*   *   *

Sebulba reached the Podracer hangar, shut off his landspeeder, and leaped from it. Dorn, still hanging to the bottom of the landspeeder, tracked Sebulba by watching his feet.

Three of Sebulba's accomplices met him, and they all headed for the hangar.

Dorn rolled to the ground and crawled out from beneath the landspeeder. He stared at the hangar, fear rising in him. He could hear the engines of a Podracer whining.

Get out of there! he wanted to warn Anakin. *Hurry!*

*   *   *

Sebulba and his henchmen—the Dug, the Sakiyan tracker, and a giant Abyssin cyclops—rushed toward the hangar. The huge machine bore down on them. Sebulba shouted in terror.

Most of them leaped aside, but the stupid cyclops pulled its blaster rifle, rushed forward, and took aim.

Anakin boosted the throttle. The Podracer gained speed.

CHAPTER EIGHT

Gondry was a stupid giant. He knew that. He was never a fast thinker. He saw the Podracer bearing down on him, and decided to fire his weapon.

But the Podracer sped up.

He was only vaguely aware of its speed. With only one eye, he had terrible depth perception. He couldn't really judge how fast something was moving toward him. Smoke from an exploded droid hung like an oily fog, and flaming debris drifted in the air.

But what Gondry saw most was the searing light of the Podracer's energy binders.

He knew what happened when you touched them. He hadn't fired his blaster when the binders slammed into him.

For a split second, he was aware that every muscle in his body tingled. All of his bones felt as if they'd turned into rubber. His legs collapsed under him.

Then the pod soared over him just as the huge engines battered through the walls.

The walls shattered into rubble. Part of the roof collapsed. The force of the impact threw Gondry thirty meters. He landed clear of the rubble, out in the street, and lay blinking up into Tatooine's double suns.

* * *

Djas Puhr had run toward the building when he heard the huge Podracer swerve out of its docking bay and head straight toward them.

He was still blinded by the sunlight. But he managed to throw himself to the ground before the others did.

The Podracer blew through the doors and screamed into the streets.

Djas Phur leaped up and drew his blaster. With one shot, he could blow the fuel tank!

Dorn leaped into the driver's seat of the landspeeder as the Podracer hurled through the walls of the hangar, spewing rocks and dust.

The Sakiyan managed to throw himself on the ground, then roll to his feet and draw his blaster. Meanwhile, Sebulba had turned and run back toward his landspeeder.

Dorn slammed his foot on the throttle, and the landspeeder shot straight ahead.

Bam! He knocked the Sakiyan down and veered away from Sebulba. In a flash Dorn was driving the stolen landspeeder home—he swerved around an astonished bantha. Crowds of people shouted and dived for cover.

He glanced over his shoulder. Sebulba drew his blaster, fired once at Dorn's back, and screamed in rage. But the shot went high. Dorn veered around a corner.

Sebulba wouldn't get a second chance.

*　　*　　*

Though his people are hard to kill, Gondry felt terrible after getting run over by the Podracer. When Djas Puhr came up shouting, "Are you alive?" Gondry had to think for a long time before he answered, "I guess."

*　　*　　*

When the Podracer pounded through the hangar wall, Khiss had been running for cover.

He was never quite sure how it happened, but he ducked for a split second and managed to avoid getting caught in the beam of the energy binders.

One engine burst through the wall to his right. If he'd managed to duck just a bit more, he'd have escaped the mess altogether.

As it was, the huge engines slowed dramatically as they slammed into the wall.

Most Podracer engines would have never made it through. But Sebulba had long ago reinforced the housing on his engines. They were *designed* to ram into other Podracers. Those huge engines were weapons, and seldom did a race go by when Sebulba didn't take out one of his foes with them.

But this time, the huge engines burst through the walls. One of the Split-X stabilizing vanes, a small wing really, caught Khiss at the waist. Suddenly he found himself hurtling down the roads of Mos Espa, clinging for his life to the fin of the Podracer.

* * *

As Anakin punched through the wall of the hangar, chunks of stone rained down behind him.

Suddenly he was in the bright streets of Tatooine, racing toward the Jawa scrap market. The buildings on the outskirts of Mos Espa reared up on both sides of the road. People screamed and ducked, while eopies leaped away in terror.

Anakin reversed thrusters and tried to slow down. He couldn't go shooting through town at 300 kilometers per hour!

He glanced back in shock at the giant he'd run over and shouted, "Sorry!"

As he looked forward again, his heart pounded in terror. The vane on his right engine had picked up a passenger!

An ugly Dug clung to it, shouting curses. He pulled himself laboriously up the vane, then tried to leap from the vane onto the top of the engine housing. His feet slipped on the housing, and he started to fall. But he grabbed onto the control arm—the joint where the Steelton control cable connected the engine—and clung there. Rage blazed in his eyes.

"I'll kill you kids!" he screamed.

Anakin swallowed back the fear in his throat and swerved to miss an eopie that wandered in front of him. If the Dug reached the Steelton cable, he could climb it like a rope, until he reached the cockpit. Then he really *would* be able to kill Anakin and Kitster.

Anakin veered left around a bantha and went screaming toward a landspeeder. The passengers all ducked just as Anakin revved the engines of the repulsorlifts, so that his Podracer gained altitude. He managed to fly over the landspeeder without knocking anyone's head off. He hit his thruster and veered right around a corner. The whole Podracer tilted at a sixty-degree angle. The right engines almost scraped the ground, and for a moment the Dug's feet actually did kick up some dust.

"Get him off of there!" Kitster screamed.

"I'm trying," Anakin shouted.

He reversed thrusters, effectively slamming on the brakes. He hoped that the Dug would be thrown forward.

But the monster clung to the control arm. He snarled in rage and began to climb onto the cables!

Anakin sped around another corner at a hundred kilometers per hour, flying over the Jawa market. With his altitude adjustment so high, he cleared the Jawas' heads nicely. But the air blowing out his jet engines blasted through the market like a hurricane, sending Jawas and all their junk flying.

The Dug was not deterred by any maneuver that Anakin tried. He was crawling closer.

Anakin reached a large empty square, slowed the thrusters, and banked hard to the right. The Podracer's engines spun in a tight circle, and the right engine dipped so low that it almost skimmed the ground.

The force on the Podracer was tremendous. Anakin circled the engines as if he were a ball at the end of a rope.

Dust and sand rose all around them in a flume that reached into the sky. It was like being at the center of a blinding sandstorm. Grit got in Anakin's teeth and nose, and Kitster closed his eyes.

But the Dug still clung to the cable arm.

What should I do? Anakin wondered.

He hit the thrusters and raced down a narrow street through the markets again. People screamed and ducked.

Anakin looked down at the control panel and spotted some buttons. He didn't know what they might do.

He pushed the right lever.

The Dug screamed in pain.

Anakin looked up. The engine was venting fire! The buttons controlled some kind of weapon.

Flames caught the Dug's legs. He shouted, let go, and went sliding over the dirt to land in a pile of wet dewback fodder.

The Dug raised his head and shook his muck-covered fist in rage.

"He ought to be glad that it put out the fire!" Kitster shouted. "Now let's get that signal jammer to Pala, before it's too late!"

* * *

Back in the hangar, Sebulba glared in anger at the escaping Podracer.

It had sailed right over his head, leaving him unharmed.

But that didn't make him any less mad.

He'd run for his landspeeder, hoping to catch the thief, but a second child had stolen it right from under his nose.

"Aaaagh!" Sebulba shouted. A mere *human* was driving his Podracer. A *child* was driving his Podracer! The kid had already blown through the wall of one building, and now was racing it through town.

Only one human in the galaxy had ever successfully piloted a Podracer, and even that particular boy had never won a race. Humans didn't have quick enough reflexes.

For half a second, Sebulba wondered if it could be Anakin Skywalker piloting his vehicle.

But it couldn't be. Anakin Skywalker wasn't stupid enough to drive a Podracer through a wall. Nor would he be so reckless as to try to fly the thing through Mos Espa.

No, it had to be some crazy, desperate kid who knew that if Sebulba caught him, he'd die a slow and agonizing death.

Maybe he wanted to go out in a blaze of glory.

Sebulba imagined his precious Podracer slamming into a massive dewback at 800 kilometers per hour. Part of him wished it would happen. At least he'd be rid of that pesky kid.

But if it did, what would he be driving for the big Boonta Eve Race?

Sebulba ran on his knuckles back into the Podracer hangar and leaped into the most likely machine: a sleek Podracer owned by a racer named Brant Rumble.

In seconds he had the engines revved. He hurtled into the streets.

*   *   *

Anakin slowed the podracer down to ninety as he roared between buldings. Even at that, he rammed into a couple of landspeeders and scraped Sebulba's engines against a building.

He couldn't afford to let people see him flying well.

"Look over there!" Kitster shouted in glee. "There's Gardulla the Hutt."

Sure enough, the sluglike creature was oozing across the road, a couple of her Gamorrean body-guards in tow. Anakin careened left toward her.

The Hutt opened her mouth wide in terror and lurched for cover.

Anakin vented flames from his left engine, searing the Hutt and her guards. Gardulla recoiled in terror.

It was time to head out of the city and ditch Sebulba's Podracer. He wouldn't be able to go far. He had to get back home soon and get the jammer to Pala, before Gardulla's henchmen identified her.

Anakin wasn't afraid for himself anymore. He'd left Sebulba's men far behind. His fear now was for Pala.

Suddenly, he heard the distant whine of a Pod-racer's engines. He recognized the sound: it was Brant Rumble's racer, roaring up behind him.

Anakin glanced back. His engines had whipped up dirt, creating a yellow haze. But through the haze he saw Brant Rumbles crimson Podracer bank a corner so hard that the Pod nearly slammed into a water tower.

Anakin opened his throttle, and the big engines bucked.

*   *   *

Sebulba raced through the Jawa market. Tailing the thieves who had stolen his slaves and his Podracer was easy.

The Podracer had knocked over market stalls, banged into walls, smashed vehicles, and otherwise created havoc. It left a cloud of thick yellow dust in the air, like a sandstorm blowing out of town.

Indeed, the children had done tremendous damage, enough so that Sebulba caught the backlash. A Trandoshan shopkeeper heard Sebulba roaring through the street. When he saw the Podracer approach, he fired a heavy blaster.

But Sebulba had excellent reflexes. He was a Dug, and the galaxy's best racer. He veered sharply, avoiding the blaster.

"Buy a bigger blaster!" he shouted.

Buildings rose on each side of the narrow street, and the odd pedestrian made the course as dangerous as any that Sebulba had ever raced. The road through town was at least as challenging as Arch Canyon.

He rounded a corner, and through a sandy haze saw the fiery engines of his own Podracer down the street, crawling at a Hutt's pace.

Stupid kids. They are puttering along.

People and animals lunged out of their path. The boys had to go slow. But the streets were clear behind them.

Sebulba whipped toward his quarry, rushing up on the Podracer from behind. The kids in their Jawa robes glanced back in terror.

The driver veered far to the left, to let Sebulba pass. Sebulba veered right. A building was there. He let his engines bank hard into the turn, so that for a moment the Podracer rose up at a seventy-degree angle, hurtling just over the surface of the dome.

Then he was past the boys. He shot ahead of them out of town, over the desert. The land opened up, a desert flat with sandstone monoliths rising here and there from the desert floor, like pillars of salt.

Sebulba spun a wide circle. He'd raised an enormous dust cloud behind him. Through the drifting yellow cloud he saw the boys still driving out of town. He grinned cruelly. He knew how to play upon the darkest fears of his foes in the racing arena.

This boy thinks he's running away from death, Sebulba realized. *What will he do if he sees it racing toward him?*

Sebulba opened up his throttle, and aimed Brant Rumble's Podracer straight at his own.

*   *   *

Anakin stared ahead toward the edge of town and gritted his teeth. Through clouds of yellow dust that drifted like smoke, he saw Sebulba racing straight at him. He saw the determination in Sebulba's move.

The domes and towers of Mos Espa formed canyon walls to Anakin's right and left, walls so narrow that he could not turn his big engines around.

Ahead, the desert beckoned. The golden flats were smooth and even. Out there, he could open up the throttle and give Sebulba's Podracer its full speed.

Desperately, he wanted to get out there, to be free for just a moment. He ached for the familiar freedom he felt when he raced, the sense that he was joined to his Podracer, that the two of them were one as they hurtled above the sand. There was always a moment when the white noise of the engine seemed to go silent, when the cheering of the crowds receded, when he felt perfectly alone and at ease.

At that time, there was nothing else in the world. No pain, no fear, no desire. Just an infinite moment of feeling that, somehow, he was part of something vastly larger than himself.

"Here," Anakin said. He shoved the signal jammer into Kitster's hand. "Go get this on Pala, right now!"

"Okay!" Kitster said.

Anakin slowed, allowing his best friend to leap off the racer and duck between a couple of buildings.

Then Anakin opened the throttles wide. He was surprised at how slowly the engines responded. He'd always thought that Sebulba had the fastest Podracer in the galaxy.

But at that moment, he made a startling discovery. Sebulba didn't win by speed alone. The reinforced housing on his engines had turned them into battering rams. That's why the engines couldn't gain speed quickly!

Of course in Podracing, having battering rams for engines worked well. When driving through the narrows of someplace like Arch Canyon, or trying to make Tusken Turn, Sebulba could hold the lead in his race simply by bashing into his competitors!

But that meant that Sebulba's Podracer had a weakness, one that Anakin might be able to exploit in some future race. A Podracer with smaller, faster engines, could finesse its way around Sebulba's big killing machine.

Anakin would not have guessed before that he could find the weaknesses of other Podracers' machines by having just a moment at the controls.

Anakin wanted to make a race of it now. But he knew that he shouldn't take the machine to top speed.

It would be dumb to try. Humans were not supposed to be able to Podrace. If Anakin dared to take Sebulba's racer to top speed, Sebulba would figure out who was driving.

The only way to win *this* match would be to slow down.

The engines roared. The sound echoed from the city walls as the Podracer swept through the narrow streets. Wind blasted Anakin's face.

Sebulba was closing on him fast, a red gleaming beast surging through clouds of drifting sand. Anakin veered right and kept his Podracer hugging that side of the street. Sebulba swerved to meet him.

Anakin fought back the fear that Sebulba wouldn't stop, that the Dug had gone mad.

No, he has to stop, Anakin thought. *He doesn't want to die, anymore than I do!* But the cruel Dug was bearing down on him.

He won't have time to veer off, Anakin thought. *We're going to crash!*

Suddenly Sebulba slowed his vehicle, raised a blaster, and fired!

The blaster bolt screamed over Anakin's head.

At that moment, time seemed to slow down. He saw the Dug bearing down on him, firing his blaster, and Anakin knew that Sebulba wouldn't hit him— either with the weapons, or with the other Podracer.

The Dug was aiming high on purpose, trying to scare Anakin without damaging his Podracer. But if Sebulba dared crash into him on Brant Rumble's racer, it would shatter in a million pieces with Sebulba in it.

No, Sebulba was only bluffing. He knew that if he could get Anakin to stop, or to pull over, or to crash, Sebulba would have him.

But Anakin could turn the tables on the wily Dug. He could turn this contest from a game of bluff into a *real* jousting match!

He feinted to the left, as if he would swerve back into the middle of the street. As he did, he hit the thrusters, and reached down to the floor, grabbing Sebulba's racing goggles and spanners.

Sebulba saw the boy veer into the middle of the street. The Dug's mouth opened wide in terror. The boy was going to kill them both!

Sebulba did not want to die, or destroy his own Podracer.

Worse than the unexpected maneuver, the kid had suddenly ducked his head, so that he couldn't see to evade Sebulba's racer.

Perhaps the boy expected to die, and didn't want to see the moment coming. Or maybe he was afraid he'd get shot if he poked his head above the dashboard.

"Aaaagh!" Sebulba shouted.

He aimed his blaster over the duraplex windscreen of Brant Rumble's Podracer and shot at the ground in front of the boy.

Sebulba swerved to his far left. The engines twisted on their energy binders as the Dug banked against the side of a dome.

The two Podracers hurtled toward each other, engines screaming.

There's not enough room to pass! Sebulba realized.

Suddenly the boy popped his head back up, hurled something, and banked to the left.

The Podracers had just enough room to clear each other on the right.

But something was falling through the air!

The cunning Dug recognized his own goggles and metal spanners, just as the jet engines on Brant Rumble's racer sucked them all in.

The right engine ground to a halt and took a nose-dive into the hardpan of Mos Espa Spaceport. Dirt and soil sprayed high into the air and the whole city shuddered with the sound of the exploding engine.

The Steelton control cable snapped off at the engine arm. The remaining engine hurtled on, dragging the cockpit behind it at five hundred kilometers per hour.

Sebulba fought the controls. Without two engines to keep the cockpit stable, his pod swung on its lone cable like a pendulum. The pod grazed a fruit dealer's shop to the left, slammed wide over to the right, smashed into a big cleaning droid, and veered back left.

Sebulba reversed thrusters on his single engine and killed the repulsor-lift motor for his Podracer. The cockpit dropped into the dust, becoming a dead weight that dragged behind the remaining engine like an anchor.

When the Podracer finally stopped, a cloud of dust rose in the street so thick that Sebulba couldn't see the path behind him.

The kids he'd been chasing were long gone.

He glared through the dust.

"I'm not done with you yet!" he growled.

At this point, readers who chose to follow the adventure in the Star Wars Adventure Game Book can return to the novel *The Hunt for Anakin Skywalker.*

CHAPTER NINE

Gardulla the Hutt was in a killing mood when she and her henchmen reached Madam Vansitt's Charm Academy. The suns were sailing down in the sky, and it was the end of a long, nasty day.

The damage that Madam Vansitt's slave had done to Gardulla's fortress was tremendous. And if the story was true, one of the very slaves who had damaged her fort and stolen her slaves had also had the audacity to nearly run her over!

Once inside the Academy doors, Gardulla studied the decor. It was all very feminine—fine painted silks decorating the walls, a pleasant perfume in the air.

Gardulla oozed into the office, and screamed at the top of her lungs, "Vansitt, get over here now!"

Madam Vansitt rushed from the back of some classroom. The girl spies she was training came to the doorway and peeked out nervously.

"How may I help you?" Madam Vansitt asked. Madam Vansitt herself was a stunning beauty—for a human woman, Gardulla thought. She was quite heavy—enough so that the rolls of fat hanging from her cheeks completely obscured her neck. And her bust and waistline were large enough to give her a pleasing, rounded shape. Indeed, very few humans were fortunate enough to look so much like Hutts.

"I'll get straight to the point," Gardulla said. "One of your girls broke into my place last night. I want her—now!"

"One of *my* girls?" Madam Vansitt asked, her mouth dropping in surprise. "Who would do such a thing?"

"Pala Kwi'teksa," Gardulla said. "One of your Twi'leks." Gardulla saw several Twi'lek girls through the doorway.

"Pala?" Madam Vansitt asked. "The slave I bought from you?"

"Point her out to me," Gardulla demanded.

Madam Vansitt glanced behind her. "Why, she's not here. I let her go a couple of hours ago. She was to be sold tomorrow, so I told her to say good-bye to her friends. I—I expect her shortly."

Gardulla studied the woman. Madam Vansitt was a capable teacher, a cruel woman, and smart. Gardulla had always respected her. But for a moment, she wondered if the teacher wasn't somehow in league with the pupil.

"Well," Gardulla said. "Isn't that convenient!"

"We can track her, though," Madam Vansitt said. She went to a desk and pulled out a portable slave tracker—a small electronic notebook. She punched some buttons and called up an image of Pala. The image was old, showing the girl as she would have looked five years ago, when Vansitt had bought her. Gardulla didn't recognize the child. She bought and sold far too many slaves to bother remembering their names or faces.

With the image on the display screen, Madam Vansitt pushed a button. A map should have appeared, with a red glowing dot to show where the slave was hiding. Instead, all that came up was a screen image scrambled by static.

Gardulla glared at the screen. "Smart girl," she said. "She's hiding next to a signal jammer."

Gardulla glanced at Madam Vansitt to see her reaction. The huge woman wore a tight-lipped smile. She said, "She *is* a smart girl. But she can't stay hidden forever. Would you like me to blow her up? The jammer might not be able to block the incoming command."

Gardulla considered. This girl was the only link she had to the other slaves who had broken into her palace. If she killed the child now, the others might go free. Normally, Gardulla would have waited. But she was in a killing mood.

"Please do," Gardulla said.

Madam Vansitt pushed another button. She held her breath for a moment afterward, as if listening for a distant explosion.

CHAPTER TEN

That evening as the suns set above Tatooine, Anakin crept down the narrow streets to Jira's apartment.

Rumors had been circulating through town all day: Jawas had stolen Sebulba's Podracer and driven it like mad through the streets. A scan showed that Pala the Twi'lek had helped steal Gardulla's slaves the previous night, and even now Gardulla was trying to track the girl.

It seemed to Anakin that his whole world was coming apart.

As he entered Jira's barren apartment, he saw Jira and two other furtive figures hiding in the shadows: Kitster and Dorn.

Pala was noticeably absent.

Jira looked up at Anakin, and said softly, "Sit down."

Anakin sat on the floor and looked up at Jira. Few lights were on in the apartment, only the running lights from a couple of machines. Her silver hair glowed dimly, but he could not see her face well.

"The news is not all good," Jira said. "A friend has made some contacts, and a ship will touch down tomorrow night. But we must have the money for the Ghostling children by then. And your friend cannot get caught between now and tomorrow. Is she safe?"

Kitster had taken the signal jammer to Pala. He only hoped it would work like it was supposed to.

"She sure is," Kitster said. "I hid her in the last place that Gardulla would look: With the Ghostling children in Gardulla's fortress. I left her there an hour ago."

"She was all right?" Dorn asked. "I heard that Gardulla made Madam Vansitt detonate her transmitter."

"She's fine," Kitster said. "Anakin's signal jammer works!"

A wave of relief washed over Anakin. He'd saved Pala's life—for now.

Dorn said, "Gardulla took a seeker droid to Pala's room and got her scent. They're hunting for her now. But we put enough perfume on her so that the seeker ought to be fooled. Then we scattered her clothes in the market. Jawas carried them off in a hundred directions! The seeker ought to be chasing them for days."

"Shhh…enough," Jira said. She put a dark finger to her lips. "Speak no more about this. I am glad you have her safe. You have done much to save her. But we must do more."

Anakin reached into the pocket of his shirt, pulling out all of his credit chips and coins. "Will this help?" He laid the money in a pile on the floor.

Jira looked at it gratefully. "Every little bit helps."

Kitster and Dorn pulled out their own money and set it down. "I can get more," Dorn promised.

"Get all that you can," Jira told them. "We'll need every bit of it."

Anakin hurried home, feeling frightened. Just after sunset on Tatooine, Mos Espa reached its busiest peak, as people came out of the buildings into the cool night air.

He watched for seekers behind him, and for Sakiyan trackers in dark clothes. But he'd taken some precautions. He'd smeared himself with a hubba gourd. That would mask his scent, even from a Sakiyan. He reached home without incident.

Once inside, he found his mother working on a droid for her friend. She glanced up at him. There was more than suspicion in her brown eyes. He saw pain and fear.

"Did you hear the news about your friend Pala?" she asked.

Anakin's heart thudded in his chest. "What news?" he asked. For a minute he imagined that she would tell him that Pala had been caught.

"Gardulla the Hutt is searching for her. She and some other children tried to help free some of Gardulla's slaves."

She didn't ask if Anakin was one of those children. But her eyes bore into him.

"They weren't Gardulla's slaves," Anakin said. "They're just poor kids that Sebulba stole from their parents."

"Do you have any money?" his mother asked.

"No," Anakin said. "I gave it all away."

She nodded, then went back to work on her droid.

She knows, Anakin thought. *My mother knows that the slaves are collecting money to help smuggle Pala off-planet.*

He wondered how many times before she might have given money to help win someone's freedom. At that moment, he felt as if he loved her more than ever before.

Anakin went to her and began sorting through some tools, so that he could help her finish the droid repairs.

"No," his mother said. "You've had a long day. Try to get some sleep."

Anakin went to his room and lay on his bed. He thought about Pala, hiding in Gardulla's fortress, in the huge pleasure garden.

He wondered if she would be able to sleep there, tonight, among the weird trees.

He imagined that she would be lying with the Ghostling children, cuddling them, trying to give them comfort.

Anakin rolled over on his bed and felt the strange cube in his pocket. He took it out and laid it in the cubbyhole above his headboard.

He fell asleep with his clothes on.

In a dream, he was in a huge room, shouting for help. He banged on the walls, trying to get out. He thought it might be Gardulla's fortress, but the high walls were square, and the roof had no transparent dome overhead. He wasn't at Gardulla's. He was inside the cube!

He could see no doors or windows, no way to escape his prison. "Help me!" he cried. "Help me get free!" He pounded on walls of cool gray metal.

"No one can help you," an evil voice whispered. "No one can help you. You must open the cube!"

"How?" he shouted. "How do I open it?"

"From the inside," the mysterious voice whispered.

Anakin started, found himself awake on his bed. It was late at night. The mysterious voice was ringing in his ears, and his heart was pounding.

He'd heard the voice, he felt sure. It wasn't a dream. It had been too real to be a dream.

But in the darkness he couldn't detect any movement nearby. No one was in the room with him, hovering above his bed.

From memory, Anakin tried to recall where the sound had come from.

The voice had spoken to him from above his bed, he was sure. It had come from the cubbyhole.

He reached up, felt for the strange cube that lay there. He grasped it in the dark and felt its square edges. Somehow, he was disappointed. He'd thought that maybe it would have opened itself, like a flower blooming. But it was still closed.

"Did you say something?" he whispered to the cube. "Did you talk to me? Are you trapped in there?"

He listened hard, and this time he thought maybe he could hear the voice answer. Or maybe it was more of a feeling that there was an answer. *Yes. I called to you.*

"How can I let you out?" Anakin whispered.

From the inside, the voice seemed to whisper.

Anakin held the box up and squinted at it. He wasn't sure if he really felt an answer. Was it possible that he could open the box, that he could find a way to open it from the inside?

And if so, what would the box contain? A tiny alien perhaps, some creature so small that it could live for a thousand years trapped in that box, trying to get out.

It seemed only barely possible.

I'm going crazy, Anakin thought. *That is what's giving me these dreams. I'm caught in a trap, and Pala and all my friends with me. No wonder I'm dreaming about being trapped inside of boxes.*

Yet even as he considered these doubts, he noticed that the cube was warmer than the night air, as if it generated a tiny amount of heat.

Live creatures give off heat, he realized.

CHAPTER ELEVEN

In lavish quarters, the great lord Jabba entertained his guest, the Podracer Sebulba. Musicians played their whining instruments, and dancing girls writhed before his throne. Chefs were bringing in trays of food.

"Why do you look so glum?" Jabba demanded as he pulled a large effrikim worm from a tray. "Did the children do that much damage to your Podracer?"

"No, O Great One," Sebulba said. "It will be fixed in time for the trial races the day after tomorrow."

"Brant Rumble's racer didn't fare as well, I hear," Jabba laughed.

Sebulba got even madder. He'd have to pay Brant Rumble for wrecking his Podracer. These kids were costing him money!

Sebulba growled. "We wasted a whole day trying to catch these monsters!"

"Perhaps you rely too much on technology, and not enough on your wits."

"What do you mean?" Sebulba asked. He looked up at the huge Hutt expectantly. Jabba was one of the greatest crime lords in the galaxy, and was filled with evil wisdom.

"I mean that these children who escaped from you won't get off of Tatooine without help—the help of adults, the help of other slaves."

"We've put a bounty on the children," Sebulba said. "Any slave would be foolish not to grab for it."

"Hmmm..." Jabba reflected. "Money may not be enough. I suggest that you try a different tactic. Send a spy to get the information you need—a spy who can gain the confidence of children."

"A spy?" Sebulba asked.

"I have just such a spy at hand, in training," Jabba said. "Let me get him for you."

Jabba glanced at one of his assistants, a droid torturer. "Go and fetch my young Bothan spy, Dorn. He'll find these children."

The droid turned and stalked away on its metal limbs.

"Are you *sure* your spy can find these kids?" Sebulba asked.

"He'll find a way—if I give him the proper encouragement," Jabba said.

"What's that?" Sebulba asked.

"I'll kill him if he fails."

Sebulba chuckled at the idea. Jabba laughed, too, his huge stomach shaking. The big booming guffaws echoed through the palace.

They had no doubt they would soon find the trespassers...and punish them accordingly.

NEXT ADVENTURE:
CAPTURE ARAWYNNE